The Postbox Topper

Liz Hedgecock

WHITE
RHINO
BOOKS

ISBN-13: 979-8876954244

*To the crafters, who knit, crochet and make
the world brighter, one stitch at a time*

1

'I'm so glad you decided to come tonight,' said Vix.

'Mmm.' Julie concentrated on picking her way along the pavement while Vix sailed on ahead, occasionally stopping for her to catch up. The path to the library wasn't well lit at the best of times, and she was worried about frost and slippery patches.

'I'm sure you'll enjoy Hooked on Yarn. Everyone does – I can't wait for Thursdays. There are older people too: not just my age. It's a shame you haven't been before.'

'I don't think I was in the right frame of mind,' Julie replied.

'No, I suppose not, what with— But it'll do you good to start going out again.' Vix gave her a friendly pat on the arm. 'It must be, what, eighteen months?'

'Nearly two years.'

'Gosh, time flies, doesn't it? Not that— Anyway,

1

here we are.' Vix ushered Julie in. 'This is the library.'

'I do live in Meadley, you know, and I use the library.' She popped in most weekends to borrow books, usually mysteries, and would often chat to the librarian on duty.

Vix sailed towards the desk. 'This is my friend Julie. She's coming to Hooked on Yarn.'

Corinne, who often chatted to Julie about the last book she had borrowed, raised her eyebrows. 'Hooked on Yarn, eh?'

'I've probably forgotten everything I ever knew about knitting,' said Julie. 'And I never learned to crochet. But I'm willing to give it a go, and Vix assures me I'll enjoy it.'

'I'm sure you will,' said Corinne, smiling. 'You know the way, Vix.'

'Yes, let's go through.' Vix shepherded Julie towards the space to the side of the main library which was used for talks and activities. Today, the tables had been pushed into the middle and sitting around them was a group of women, unpacking balls of yarn from their bags and chatting.

'Hello, everyone!' cried Vix. 'I've brought a new recruit. This is Julie. We work together.'

'Hi, Julie,' said a fortysomething woman with winged glasses and a long brown bob. Julie was sure she'd seen her in the village coffee shop, reading. She was wearing a red and white striped sweater appliquéd with knitted navy flowers. Julie wondered how on earth she washed it without the colours running. 'I'm Lucy. Are you local?'

'Yes, I live on Beech Lane, near the primary school. I've lived in Meadley for three years.'

'Ahhh, you're an incomer, then.' She grinned. 'Not that I believe in all that snobby "My family have been here for generations" rubbish, but you know what some people are like.'

'Idiots,' said a young woman with pink hair and a T-shirt which proclaimed *KNITTING NEEDLES ARE A WEAPON*. 'I'm Tegan, by the way.'

'Hello, Tegan.' Julie peered at the mass of pink wool dangling from Tegan's crochet hook. 'What are you making?'

'It's a uterus,' said Tegan. 'Anatomically correct. It's an art piece.'

'Tegan's our resident angry young woman,' said Vix, grinning. 'Aren't you, Tegan?'

'I don't see why crocheting a uterus makes me an angry person,' said Tegan, looking mutinous. 'I mean, obviously it isn't just *any* uterus—'

A woman in a Peruvian jacket rushed in and flung herself into the nearest chair. 'Sorry I'm late: I was dealing with a tantrum at home. For some reason, Jake now can't eat anything that's touched another type of food on the plate. Not good when you've given

3

them fish fingers and chips with peas and sweetcorn.'

Tegan looked horrified. 'Don't tell me you had to separate the peas from the sweetcorn, Natalie.'

Natalie shrugged. 'What do you think?'

'Female oppression,' muttered Tegan.

The woman sitting at the far corner of the table cleared her throat. 'As everyone's here, shall we get on?' She was somewhere in her thirties, with cropped dark hair and a chunky sweater. Julie wondered if she'd made it herself.

Various nods, and murmurs of 'Yes, Miriam.' Even Tegan put down her crochet and paid attention. *We have a group leader,* thought Julie.

'I've been thinking,' said Miriam. 'We did really well with our crocheted poppies for Remembrance Day, and then the stall at the Christmas fair. Maybe we could do a project together. Something for the village.'

'How do you mean?' asked Vix.

'I know what we could do,' said Tegan. 'Yarn bombing.'

'Yarn bombing?' Vix laughed. 'What the heck is that?'

'When you knit covers for bollards,' said Tegan. 'And wrap lamp posts and trees and… Stuff like that. Guerilla knitting.'

'Ooh, I've never knitted a gorilla,' said a trim woman with short grey hair and smiling eyes.

Tegan laughed. 'Hang on, Bernie, I'll show you.' She pulled out her phone, and after a bit of searching, held it up.

Julie saw a tree with its trunk and branches wrapped in red and green squares. Baubles dangled from woollen chains. 'That looks complicated,' she said, faintly.

'Don't worry, Jules,' said Vix. 'You could do a couple of squares, I'm sure. Anyway, that's a Christmas one, and it's almost February.'

'That was just an example,' said Tegan. 'We could make a difference. We could knit big stand-up arrows and point them at the potholes. Or knit a life-size version of our MP and put him in the stocks.'

'Or we could start with something a bit smaller,' said Miriam. 'Like a postbox topper.'

'Oh yes, those are cool,' said Natalie. 'I've seen them on the internet. There was a snowman one in Meadhurst at Christmas.'

'What do the rest of you think?' said Miriam.

'It's a bit tame,' said Tegan. 'We could do something really radical.'

'Which would probably be taken down,' said Miriam, 'Why don't we do something people will like, and go from there?'

Tegan thought this over. 'I suppose,' she said, with a sigh. 'I do get what you mean, but . . . it's annoying.'

'I know,' Miriam soothed. 'Does anyone have any

other ideas for a group project?'

'I'm still tempted by the gorilla,' said Bernie, 'but a postbox topper seems a good idea. It's just like doing a round hat, isn't it, and then decorating it?'

'That's it,' said Miriam. 'OK, let's pick a theme, then we can look at our supplies and get started.' Julie suspected making a postbox topper had been Miriam's intention all along.

Miriam's eyes met hers and she jumped. 'Julie – it is Julie, isn't it?'

'That's right,' said Julie. She felt unaccountably nervous.

Miriam smiled at her. 'Are you a knitter or a crocheter?'

'I'm not sure I'm either,' said Julie. 'I never learnt to crochet, but I can knit a bit.'

'I'll get someone to take you under their wing.'

Five minutes later, Julie had been handed over to Lucy, who supplied her with a ball of wool and a crochet hook and instructed her on how to make a chain. 'After all,' she said, 'you won't know whether you prefer knitting or crochet until you've tried them both.'

'Did you make the flowers on your jumper?' asked Julie, pausing in her battle to keep the yarn on her hook and the links of the chain the same size.

'I did. And the jumper.' Lucy put her head on one side. 'I'm surprised I haven't seen you about, since you're local.'

'I work in Meadborough, so I'm not around during the day.'

'Oh,' said Lucy, and left it at that, for which Julie was grateful. 'It's nice that you found us.'

'Well, Vix brought me.' Julie felt her face grow warm. *You sound like a child who has to be taken places*, she thought to herself. *Honestly, Julie.*

'Yes, but you still came.' Lucy put down the blanket square she was crocheting and gently inspected Julie's chain. 'That's pretty good. Want to learn something else?'

Julie found herself smiling. 'Yes, if that's OK.'

Lucy laughed. 'Of course it is!'

Someone touched Julie's shoulder and she jumped. 'Are you getting on all right?' asked Vix, her brown eyes round with concern. 'I'm sorry, I would have come over before, but I couldn't get away. Catching up, you know.' From her needles dangled a blue and white striped sock sized for a very large foot.

'I – I think so.' Julie looked at Lucy for confirmation.

'She's doing really well, Vix,' said Lucy.

Vix crouched next to Julie and put a hand on her arm. 'You're sure? You don't feel overwhelmed or anything?'

'I'm fine,' said Julie, wishing Vix would disappear.

'Oh good! I'm so pleased! I wasn't sure how you'd

get on, seeing as you don't get out much. Well done you.' Vix beamed at her. 'Better go, Bernie wants a word.' And Vix strode off, the sock bobbing up and down on its needles as if it was walking too.

Some time later, as Julie was embarking on crocheting a ring, Miriam clapped her hands. 'Sorry to be schoolmarmy, but I've been doing a stocktake of the yarn cupboard. We have lots of pale green, various shades of yellow, a fair bit of white and a ball each of various other colours. We're completely out of red after doing all those poppies, obviously. Does anyone have any bright ideas? I mean, we could buy more yarn, but I like the idea of using what we have.'

'Green and yellow,' said Bernie, meditatively. 'A fruit bowl with apples and bananas?'

'We could do an abstract,' said Tegan. 'Then anything goes.'

'We could,' said Miriam, who looked as if her patience was being tested. 'But as this is our first postbox topper, it's important that people can tell what it is.'

Julie eyed the flowers on Lucy's jumper and raised her hand to the level of her shoulder. 'We could, um, maybe do something with spring flowers? A green cover, with daffodils and daisies and . . . other ones.'

'Yes!' said Natalie. 'And rabbits.'

'And crocuses,' said Lucy.

Tegan sighed. 'I suppose you want to put a rainbow

8

and fluffy clouds on it too, or spring lambs.'

'Definitely lambs,' said Miriam. 'Right, who's in favour of a spring-themed postbox topper?'

Everyone except Tegan raised their hand.

Tegan surveyed the group, rolled her eyes and raised hers too. 'We should do a witchy one for Halloween,' she said.

'I have no objection,' said Miriam, 'so long as it's a majority vote.'

A knock on the wall made everyone turn their heads. 'Sorry to interrupt,' said Corinne, 'but I'm closing in five minutes.' She surveyed them. 'You're very pleased with yourselves. Have you been plotting?'

Everyone looked blank. 'Us, plotting?' said Miriam. 'You must be thinking of some other group of women.'

Corinne's eyes narrowed. 'Whatever it is, it'll have to wait until next week.'

'It won't,' said Miriam. 'Everyone, decide what you'd like to crochet and put it in the WhatsApp group. Now, we'd better pack up. Needles down, folks.'

'So there's a WhatsApp group?' said Julie, as she and Vix picked their way along the path.

'Yes, shall I add you?'

'Um… I'm not on WhatsApp.'

'Oh,' said Vix. 'Never mind, I can keep you up to

speed. We see each other almost every day at work, don't we?'

'Yes, of course,' said Julie, and resolved to get WhatsApp onto her phone when she got home. That, and find a YouTube tutorial on how to crochet flowers.

2

Natalie: *I'm doing two lambs and a five-bar gate. If I can, I'll wire the lambs so they're jumping over it.*

Lucy: *I'll have a go at some daffodils. Is it cheating if we wire the stems? Or do I just do the heads?*

Bernie: *I'll do the bonnet. Seeing as gorillas aren't native to this county :(*

Tegan: *If I knit battery hens you'll complain, so I'll do ducks.*

Miriam: *Lovely, it's all coming together. Who's left, and what do you want to do?*

Vix: *I'll make cute yellow chicks. Jules, what about you? Could you do crocuses?*

Julie put down her phone. This was what she had been dreading. She could hear her heart thumping. *I have no idea where to start.* Then she realised that if

11

she said nothing, Vix and the others might take that as agreement. She picked up the phone and began to type. *I think I can crochet some simple daisies, if that's OK. I have a ball of white wool so I only need yellow. I'm not ready for crocuses yet.*

Vix: *I'm sure someone could teach you to do a crocus next meeting. Or I could show you in our lunch breaks.*
Miriam: *Daisies would be great, Julie. I'll take on the crocuses. Vix, can you pass on yellow wool to Julie?*

OK, Julie replied. She was about to close the app when a thought struck her. After a bit of clicking, she found the group's details. There was a mute option, which she clicked. *There. If someone from the group asks, I can always say I don't check my phone very often, or that I must have muted it by accident.* She closed her eyes and exhaled, then got up and put the kettle on.

She had told Vix at work that she would make her own way to the group next time. 'It's out of your way, Vix, and I'll be quite safe walking. The road's well lit.'

'Are you sure?' said Vix. 'No one's really safe anywhere. The things you hear about that happen in broad daylight—'

'I'll be fine,' said Julie.

On the evening of the meeting Julie got ready in good time, dressing warmly, with sensible shoes. She packed her crochet hook, yarn and the daisies she had made already in a little pouch. She was locking up when the front door of the adjoining cottage opened and her neighbour Neil appeared. 'Hello Julie, off out?' His longish, unruly brown hair made him look rather like a curious lion.

'I am, as it happens.' Julie tried the handle of her door, just to be sure. Of course, it was locked.

'Going somewhere nice?'

'Yes, to a knitting and crochet group at the library.' The cuff of Neil's baggy green jumper was coming undone. Julie wondered whether she should suggest he accompany her to get it fixed.

Neil's eyebrows knitted in a humorous frown. 'Knitting and crochet? Isn't that what grannies do?'

Julie considered how to reply. There were so many things she could say, none particularly polite. 'I'm in my fifties, Neil. Maybe I'm just getting in early.'

His smile vanished. 'Oh no, I didn't mean— What I meant was that you're not old enough for that sort of thing.'

'I enjoy it. It's nice to chat to people.'

'You could chat to me,' said Neil. 'I'm only next door, if you want a conversation.'

What on earth would we talk about? thought Julie.

Whether the fence needs repainting? The state of Meadley's roads? Offers at the local supermarket? 'Thanks, Neil, I'll remember that. Anyway, must get on.'

'When will you be back?' asked Neil. 'So I can check you're home safe.'

'I'm not likely to go missing, Neil!' Julie laughed. 'And I doubt I'll get lost.' She raised a hand in farewell and walked down the path. *What a fuss over a trip to the library. Anyone would think I was off around the world.*

***

She arrived at the library to find Vix standing outside. Vix waved frantically. '*There* you are!'

Julie checked her watch. 'It's five to, Vix. I'm early.'

'Yes, well, I worry. Let's go in.' She steered Julie through the door and straight into the meeting space as if Julie might break free and make a run for it. 'Here she is!' she announced, then took the nearest chair and began unpacking her bag.

Julie was somewhat dismayed to see that everyone had made considerable progress with their parts of the project. Natalie had two lambs propped up in front of her and was working on a third. Lucy had a row of daffodils. Tegan had knitted a duck and drake with menacing, beady eyes, and a pair of ducklings swam along the table behind them. Bernie was hard at work

14

on what looked like an enormous beret.

'Hello, Julie,' said Miriam, setting down her crochet. 'There's a spare seat over by Bernie.'

'Oh, Jules can squish in next to me,' said Vix, scraping her chair. But Julie was already making her way round the table. She sat down, put her bag on her lap and pulled out the pouch. 'They aren't great,' she said apologetically, 'but I've made a start.' She set out the daisies.

'Oh, they're cute,' said Lucy. 'And very regular. When I first began crocheting, everything began really tight then loosened until it was twice the size.'

Julie peered at everyone else's creations. 'Should I do bigger ones?' she asked. 'I wasn't sure what size to make, so I went small to be on the safe side.'

'You could do,' said Miriam. 'So long as they're not the same size as the lambs.'

'Although you'd be making a great point about GM crops,' said Tegan, and Lucy sighed.

There was much less conversation than at the previous meeting, because people were focused on their work. In some ways that was nice, thought Julie. It was relaxing not to have to think of small talk or reply to questions she found difficult, even if they weren't meant to be. Being social without being social.

An hour in, a chair scraped and everyone looked up. Miriam was inspecting the table. 'Wow,' she said,

'We're practically there. The topper itself is done, we've got lambs, a gate, ducks, chicks and lots of flowers. It'll be spectacular.'

'If you whizz the completed bits my way,' said Bernie, 'I'll arrange them on the topper, ready for sewing.'

Julie reflected on how nice it was to have someone else monitoring a project for a change, then stared as various woollen items shot past her. 'It can't be finished,' she said.

Miriam grinned. 'It's amazing what we can do when we put our minds to it.'

Bernie was arranging their contributions on the topper, which was in shades of green with a blue pond in the middle. 'Lovely,' she said. 'Can you pass me your daisies, Julie?'

Julie picked up her flowers and handed them to Bernie. Pushing them across the table as the others had done felt rude. 'I'll finish the one I'm on,' she said, and continued to crochet.

A few minutes later, Bernie clapped her hands. 'Everyone happy?'

'Oh yes,' said Miriam. 'I think you're ready to sew.'

Julie finished her daisy, worked in the end and looked up. What she saw already seemed complete. The topper was bordered with flowers. Ducks swam in the pond, chicks roamed the fields and the lambs watched one of their number hurdle a five-bar gate. 'That's amazing,' she said. 'I don't suppose you need this daisy.'

'Always room for one more,' said Bernie. She held out her hand for the daisy and put it between a daffodil and a crocus.

'Are you all right to make it up, Bernie?' asked Miriam. 'Once that's done, we can put it on.' She leaned forward and lowered her voice. 'Under cover of darkness.'

Lucy laughed. 'Is that necessary?'

Tegan tutted. 'The whole point of yarn bombing is that it's secret. It comes in the night, when no one expects it.'

Natalie giggled. 'I can see the papers. *The village was ambushed by three fluffy lambs, some chicks and a flock of evil ducks.*'

Bernie stood up and took a picture of the laid-out topper with her phone. 'There, now I've got something to work with. I reckon I can get this done tonight, if I push.'

'Let me know when you have,' said Miriam. 'If you don't mind, I'll pick it up and pop it on once the village is quiet. I doubt anyone will be out past midnight on a school night, and it would be great to get it on for the weekend. I'll put a message in the WhatsApp group when it's in place.'

Vix insisted on walking Julie home. 'Aren't you

glad I persuaded you to come to the group now?' she asked.

Julie smiled. 'Yes, it's nice. Although... Is it always so full on?'

'It can be busy,' said Vix. 'That's part of the fun.'

I suppose it is, thought Julie. *If you like that sort of thing.* She had spent so much time in the last few years struggling to stay calm and not be upset that voluntarily stepping into a busy environment seemed strange.

'Here we are,' said Vix, as they arrived at Julie's gate. 'Home sweet home.'

'Um, yes,' said Julie. 'Thanks for walking me home. You really didn't have to.'

She opened the gate and started down the path. The gate clicked to, and shortly afterwards Neil's front door opened. 'Returned from your knitting, then,' he said, leaning against the doorframe.

'I was crocheting,' said Julie. 'But yes.'

He waved a dismissive hand. 'Knitting, crocheting, isn't it the same?'

'It certainly is not,' snapped Vix, from the gate.

Neil drew back slightly. 'Sorry I spoke. You carry on doing whatever it is you've been doing. Don't mind me.'

'We've been doing something to benefit the village,' said Vix, drawing herself up.

'Oh yes? What would that be?'

'Never you mind,' Vix retorted. 'See you tomorrow, Jules.' She flounced off, chin in the air.

Neil snorted. 'Jules? That's a new one.'

'No one else calls me that,' said Julie, though she checked the road first to make sure Vix was too far away to hear. 'She's a work colleague.'

'Lucky you,' said Neil. 'If that's who you meet at this knitting club, I'm glad I'm not a member.'

Julie's skin prickled with irritation. 'You didn't have to come out and ask questions. Now, if you don't mind, I'm going in. It was quite a busy meeting.'

'Needles flying, were they?' Neil looked down at his own sweater.

'We're working on a project, actually.'

'Which is?' Neil ran a hand through his mop of curly hair. In Julie's opinion, it needed cutting. Jason would never have let his get as far as his collar.

She was tempted to echo Vix and say *Never you mind*, but the thought of following in Vix's footsteps put her off. 'You'll find out soon,' she said, instead. 'Good night, Neil.'

'Good night,' he said, as she found her key and put it in the lock. 'Jules.' And before she could reply, he closed his door.

***

The next morning, Julie left for work slightly early, so that she could drive through the village and see the postbox topper. It was hard to miss. Even at ten past

19

eight in the morning, three people were standing by the postbox, two with dogs, gesturing and talking. She would have liked to park the car and have a proper look, but there wasn't time. Nevertheless, a glimpse of the postbox topper, with its spring lambs and bright flowers, was more than enough to make her smile all the way to work. *I helped make that,* she thought. *I can admire it at the weekend.*

Or so she thought.

She was eating a sandwich at her desk after a morning of chasing project outputs when Vix burst in. 'I don't believe it!' she cried.

Julie froze, mid-chew. 'What is it? Is something wrong in the sales department? Don't tell me the systems are playing up ag—'

'Not sales.' Vix waved her phone. 'Haven't you seen Miriam's message?'

'No, I keep my phone on silent.' Julie fumbled in her handbag.

'Here.' Vix tapped at her phone, then shoved the screen under Julie's nose.

Unbelievable, the message read. *Less than 12 hours after I put the topper on, it's vanished. Someone must have pinched it.*

'Vandals,' said Vix. 'What a waste. The work we put in to get it done, too. I'm heading to the cafeteria to eat something naughty. Want to come?'

Julie indicated her sandwich. 'I'm a bit pushed for

time, Vix—'

'In that case, I'll let you get on.' Vix stomped off and automatically Julie took another bite of her sandwich. Now, though, it had no taste at all.

3

By two o'clock, Julie was fuming.

She wasn't sure why she felt so strongly about the postbox topper. She had gone from thinking *Honestly, some people* to *Why?* to actual rage. She sat at her desk, too furious even to concentrate on the report which her boss, Greg, had dumped on her desk, and which she was supposed to be checking for errors. Not that it was her job – she was a project coordinator, not a proofreader – but Greg always wheedled that she was so good at it that he didn't trust anyone else. The report had arrived with a sticky note on the front, on which was scrawled *Work your magic, pretty please ;-) G.*

She glanced at her half-eaten sandwich, curling at the edges, then got out her phone and unmuted the WhatsApp group.

Unsurprisingly, there was a string of replies under

Miriam's post.

Lucy: *I don't believe it! It's been up all of five minutes.*

Vix: *I know! What a shocker!*

Bernie: *What do we do? Do we make another one?*

Tegan: *What's the point? They'll probably steal that too. And you lot wonder why I get angry.*

Miriam: *We probably shouldn't jump to conclusions. Maybe someone took it off for a good reason. But I must admit that I'm annoyed.*

Julie found herself taking deep breaths to calm down. She could feel tears pricking at the back of her eyes and a lump forming in her throat. *Don't be ridiculous, Julie,* she told herself. *Why are you getting upset about a bit of wool?*

It wasn't just a bit of wool, though, was it? We put effort into that. Care. Some of us might have put love into it. And someone's taken it without a second thought.

Another message popped up.

Bernie: *You'll think I'm silly, but this makes me really sad.*

Tegan: *This is why we can't do nice things.*

23

Julie made a strange noise. *These people are the closest thing I've had to friends since – since—* She rubbed her eyes fiercely. You couldn't call a couple of knitting sessions a friendship. Vix was her best friend now, really.

She had had friends, of course, back in Barking. Then Jason had come home one night looking as if he would burst. 'Which do you want first?' he asked. 'The good news or the bad news?'

'The bad news,' Julie said, automatically. She would always rather have the bad news first and get it over with. If the good news wasn't great, at least it wouldn't make her feel worse.

He gave her a serious look. 'Are you sure?'

She shrugged. 'You know me.'

He grinned. Perhaps the bad news wouldn't be too bad. 'They're talking about downsizing the plant.'

Julie stared at him. 'Oh no. Your job isn't affected, is it?'

'It could be. Anyway, here's the good news. I heard on the grapevine that they'll be offering voluntary redundancies and relocations.' A spark danced in his blue eyes.

'What are you thinking?' she asked, suspiciously.

'Well, I considered voluntary redundancy, but I haven't been there long enough to have much of a package.'

'Ha ha.'

24

'Give over!' He chuckled. 'So I had a look at the locations of the other plants. Loads are in the back of beyond, but there's one a few miles from a place called Meadborough which could be a good fit. They have product lines similar to the one I manage, but bigger, and they make more stuff. Chances are that I might get asked to relocate there anyway, but I figured I should make the first move.'

Julie stared at him. 'Where the heck is Meadborough? What about my job? What am I supposed to do?'

'It's a nice little market town with surrounding villages, set in beautiful countryside. The sort of place we've always talked about retiring to one day. Here.' He pulled out his phone. 'There's a Wikipedia entry. Look at those hills. We could bike around the countryside together. No more London traffic.'

'I don't have a bike.'

'You could get one. Just think about it. It could be the best thing we've ever done. Meadborough has a mainline station to London, so we wouldn't be cut off from the outside world.'

'OK, I'll think about it,' said Julie.

But following that first conversation, things moved quickly. As it turned out, Jason's division was closing much earlier than he had anticipated. A month later, he had interviewed for and got an equivalent role at the Meadborough plant, and a month after that, the removal van arrived at their flat.

'From a flat to a house, eh?' Jason said, pulling her close. 'What about that?'

Jason revelled in their new home, a terraced cottage in the village of Meadley. He went for long bike rides, joined a cycling club, sampled the craft beer at his new local.

'I hardly see you nowadays,' Julie said one night, when he returned from the village.

'It's the time of year,' he said. 'There's always lots going on at Christmas. You're always welcome to come along. Lots of the cycling wives do.'

'Cycling widows, you mean. It's not really my scene. I don't fancy sitting in the corner with a glass of white wine while you talk about pedals and cleats and whether you should shave your legs or not. And before you ask, no, you shouldn't. Anyway, there's the house to get straight. Rooms to paint, stuff to fix. Plus I don't understand how the contents of our flat don't fit in an actual house. I swear it's a reverse Tardis: smaller on the inside.'

'I can always take some bits and bobs to work,' he said, 'now I've got an office of my own.'

That was where Jason had died the following September. The caretaker had come round to lock up and found him, cold and sagging in his chair. A ruptured aneurysm in his brain, according to the post-mortem. There was no way anyone could have known, since Jason had always been fit as a fiddle and had had no symptoms. *If you'd had headaches,* thought Julie, *or double vision, or anything that could have told us…*

Julie considered selling up and returning to Barking. That seemed an impossibly big task. She'd have to find a smaller flat, her post in Barking had been filled, and she had a job in Meadborough. More to the point, she couldn't face another upheaval.

She kept going to work: she found the dull routine comforting. Maintain spreadsheets, police milestones, nudge people until things got done. Besides, she'd worked at the company for less than a year. If she went missing for a few weeks, she might return to find that she had no job at all. When she came home, though, to a house now too big for her, she made a cup of tea and sank into an armchair, too sad and weary to do anything. Usually, the tea went cold. *This isn't how it was supposed to be,* she whispered sometimes.

And the friends she had promised to keep in touch with, who had sworn they would keep in touch with her? Mostly Julie let the phone ring when they called, unable to face another outpouring of sympathy, and she took herself out of cheery group chats. Gradually, because she wasn't part of their plans any more, the texts stopped coming too, except at Christmas and birthdays. Oh, and the anniversary of Jason's death.

Thinking of you xxx

In that respect, Vix had been kinder than she deserved.

She had been sitting in the cafeteria, poking at her plate of macaroni cheese and feeling thoroughly miserable, when someone said 'Mind if I join you?'

A tall, broad woman who Julie vaguely remembered from her induction was standing there with a tray. 'I'm Vix. You're Julie, aren't you?'

'That's right.'

Vix nodded towards Julie's plate. 'That looks nice.'

Julie shrugged. 'It's OK. It saves cooking at night.' She wasn't lazy and she was a reasonable cook, but the thought of planning meals for one, or cooking the quantities she always had and freezing a portion, was too depressing for words.

'I heard about your husband,' said Vix. 'I'm so sorry. What a thing to happen.'

'It was,' said Julie. 'It was terrible.' All of a sudden she was crying.

Vix banged down her tray and put an arm round her. 'It's OK, Julie. You let it out. It's fine.'

Since then, Vix had always made a point of checking in on her and making sure she was all right. She lived at the other end of Meadley with her partner, Dave, and while she wasn't exactly who Julie would have chosen for a friend, she had been very kind.

But now, for the first time in a long time, Julie felt as if she had friends.

She blinked, and looked at her phone screen. WhatsApp was still open. Before she knew it, she was typing a message.

Whoever did this ought to be ashamed of themselves. I'm going to track them down and get the postbox topper back.

Great idea! Vix responded, almost immediately.

Miriam replied perhaps a minute later. *It's good of you to suggest it, Julie, but how?*

I've read more mystery and detective books than I've had hot dinners, Julie typed. *I'll find a way.* She thought for a moment, then added: *I have my methods, Watson.*

Go Sherlock! posted Lucy.

Right, thought Julie, *I will.*

She made a list of people who might possibly steal a postbox topper. It wasn't very specific.

A jobsworth postal worker
Kids doing it for a laugh
Someone who's jealous of it

Who could that be? Julie frowned. *A disgruntled local knitter?*

How could she know for sure who had taken it? It wasn't as if anyone had been watching the postbox.

29

Surely anyone who had seen someone remove the topper would report it.

With that in mind, she rang the parish council. She didn't expect an answer, but within two rings there was a click and a friendly voice said 'Hello, Meadley Parish Council, Clerk of the Council speaking.'

'Oh, hello,' said Julie. 'I'm calling about the postbox topper that's gone missing.'

'Oh yes, I heard about the postbox topper. You say it's gone missing?'

Julie sighed. 'I don't need to ask my next question, then. I wondered if anyone had reported seeing it being taken.'

'I'm afraid not. When did this happen?'

'It had gone by one o'clock.' Miriam's message reporting the topper missing had been timestamped *12:56.*

'In that case, definitely not. I checked the answerphone when I came back from lunch. There were no messages, and you're the first person who's said anything about it. I'd suggest looking at the CCTV in the middle of the village—'

'Oh, is there CCTV?' Julie exclaimed.

'There is, but it doesn't cover the postbox. I'm really sorry, I don't think I can help.'

'Thanks for your time. I'll see what the police can do.'

'I'm not sure—' But Julie had already ended the

call.

'Good afternoon, Meadborough constabulary.'

'I wish to report… I'm not sure if it's theft or vandalism.'

The voice on the other end of the phone sounded amused. 'Surely you must know, madam.'

'A postbox topper has been stolen from the postbox in Meadley village.'

'A postbox topper.' A pause. 'What would that be?'

'You must have seen them. It's a sort of knitted hat that goes on top of a postbox. This one was decorated in a spring theme, with animals and flowers on.'

'Right.' Another pause. 'Well, you learn something every day. So this is a hat for a postbox.'

'Yes.'

'Made of wool.'

'Yes, made of wool.'

'So presumably not of high value.'

'The wool isn't, but a great deal of work went into it and—'

'I really don't think this is a matter for the police, madam. We can barely keep up with proper criminals.'

'I might have known you'd say that,' Julie said bitterly.

'If you leave your number, madam, I'll keep it on file. Then if any of our officers spot a suspicious character wearing a large spring-themed hat, we can take the appropriate action and let you know.'

Julie ended the call and slammed her phone on the desk. Then she turned it to silent mode, put it in her bag, and picked up the report she had been neglecting.

At five o'clock, having read the same page of the report several times, Julie left the office and drove to Meadley. However, she didn't go straight home. Instead, she parked in the village car park and walked round to the postbox. Unsurprisingly, it stood a few feet from the post office, which was in the middle of a small parade of shops. *Why didn't anyone see?*

She looked this way and that. A small alley ran between two of the shops – where did it lead? She walked over and peered down it, but it ended in a padlocked wooden gate. *That's a dead end, unless whoever took it has a key.* The alley divided the hardware shop and the grocer's. *Why would either of them want it?*

She turned and almost bumped into Neil. 'Sorry,' he said, then realised who she was. 'Hello. Why were you peeking in there?'

'The postbox topper our group made has been stolen,' said Julie. 'I'm trying to work out who did it.'

'The postbox topper?' Neil looked at her, then swung round to gaze at the postbox. 'Oh, I see!' He grinned. 'So that was your top-secret project?'

'It was,' Julie said, stiffly. 'Until someone pinched it. It had only been on the postbox for a few hours.

Maybe someone in the post office took it off.'

'You won't find out tonight,' said Neil. 'They shut five minutes ago.'

'Typical,' said Julie, and glared at the display of padded envelopes and hearts in the window. *Send love to someone this Valentine's Day*, a sign proclaimed.

'Well, I'll leave you to your deductions, Miss Marple,' said Neil. 'I popped into the village for carrots. Beef stew tonight.' He half-lifted a shopping bag.

'Oh, very nice,' Julie said, automatically. She had gone back to cooking at night now, having exhausted the cafeteria's limited options, but her meals tended to be simple and she never cooked any of Jason's favourites.

'See you around,' said Neil, and strode off. Julie wondered whether she should have offered him a lift. Then again, he probably felt like a walk after a day at his desk. *Besides*, she thought sourly, *he thinks the postbox topper going missing is funny. Miss Marple, indeed. He'll be laughing on the other side of his face when I catch the person who did it.*

4

At the next meeting of Hooked on Yarn, everyone seemed subdued. People said hello and exchanged pleasantries, but no one took out their work. They eyed each other, waiting.

'So, Julie, anything to feed back?' said Miriam. Her voice was casual yet kind, as if enquiring how a minor operation had gone. Removing an ingrown toenail, for instance.

'I've made enquiries,' said Julie. 'No one's reported anything to the parish council, and the police were no help.'

Tegan snorted and began to unpack the uterus she had been working on, which didn't want to come out of her bag.

'I also asked in the post office – several different people – but no one saw anything. Neither did any of the staff in that parade of shops. I've been in every shop in the village. The only thing I have managed to find out is that the postbox topper was still there at half past eleven that morning. One of the post-office workers said she saw it when she went to open the door for a customer, but when the postman came to collect from the box at noon, he asked where the topper had gone. So it disappeared between half eleven and twelve.'

'That's a narrow window,' said Miriam. 'Surely the village would have been fairly busy at that point. It was a nice day, wasn't it? For February.'

'The plot thickens,' said Lucy, and shrugged when everyone looked at her.

'I'll keep trying,' said Julie. 'At least I've narrowed it down.'

'You have,' said Miriam. 'Thanks for your hard work on this, Julie.' She sighed. 'But we have to accept that the postbox topper has probably gone for good.'

'I'll still keep trying,' said Julie. She felt her hands making fists and shoved them in her lap.

'So what do we do?' said Natalie. 'Do we make another topper, or what?'

'Let's vote on it and go with the majority,' said Miriam. 'That's the fairest thing to do. All those in favour of making another topper, raise your hands.'

Bernie's hand shot up, as did Natalie's. Lucy raised hers a few seconds later.

'I agree with you,' said Miriam. 'We should try again.' She put up her hand.

Vix looked round the room. 'I'm still annoyed about it,' she said, and raised her hand.

Tegan stared at her uterus, which was coming on nicely. 'It's not what I wanted to do in the first place,' she said. 'And I'm pretty sure that whoever pinched the first one will come back. But yeah, whatever.' She raised her hand.

Everyone looked at Julie. 'You might as well just say that you don't think I'll find the topper,' she said.

'I don't think Hercule Poirot could find this topper,' said Miriam. 'Or Inspector Morse, or anyone. There are no clues, and no leads. Anyway, we said majority vote. If you'd rather not make another topper, you can always work on something else. We won't mind.'

'Fine,' said Julie. 'As long as you know I'm against it.' She raised her hand to ear level.

'Right, motion carried.' Miriam was brisk again. 'Operation Replacement Postbox Topper is on. And this time I'll secure it so tightly that they'll need a chainsaw to get it off. That's a joke,' she added, looking around the group. 'Luckily, we still have enough yarn. Will we all do the same thing? Does anyone want to swap?'

'Could I swap with someone?' said Lucy. 'I've got a lot on at the moment and daffodils are quite fiddly.'

'I'll try, if you show me what to do,' said Julie. She regretted her words as as soon as she'd said them.

Lucy looked slightly sheepish. 'I followed a YouTube tutorial. I'll send it to the WhatsApp group. I can start you off, though.'

'Back to the killer ducks,' said Tegan, and stuffed her uterus in its bag.

***

On Friday, Julie tried to concentrate on her work, but her mind kept wandering to the postbox topper and who could possibly have taken it. Who would choose one of the busiest times of the day to steal something? And why hadn't anyone seen them?

With that in mind, she walked to the village at lunchtime on Saturday and loitered near the postbox. The village was teeming with people bringing parcels to post, getting meat from the butcher, popping into the delicatessen and heading for the coffee shop. Barely five seconds went by when someone didn't walk past the postbox. Admittedly, lots of them were talking to their companion or on their phones, but enough of them glanced curiously at Julie to convince her that anyone pinching the topper would have been spotted. Unless... Could the thief have created a psychological moment and made everyone look elsewhere? But how? Had they brought an accomplice?

Could the wind have blown it off? she thought.

Miriam said it wasn't very secure.

It would have to be a heck of a gust of wind. She checked the weather for that day. There had been a gentle breeze, at most. 'I bet Hercule Poirot never had to put up with this.'

A couple of people stared, then giggled, and Julie realised she had spoken out loud. She hurried away.

She felt peckish, but didn't want to brave the coffee shop. She had interrogated several shopkeepers, and so many people had given her odd glances that she feared they viewed her as an eccentric. Hopefully, a harmless one. *I'll stroll round the park, and go later.*

Once she got past the children laughing and screaming on the swings and slides, the park was quiet. Julie strolled along the path, musing. *If the Famous Five were investigating this, the postbox topper would probably be in a hollow tree. Or Uncle Quentin's study.*

Something rustled on her right, in what she thought of as the nature area, since it had bird boxes and a couple of feeders. A squirrel? Julie paused, listening. *Is it a sign?*

An image of bright wool protruding from a hole in a sturdy tree flashed into her mind. She left the path and tiptoed through the remains of leaves and stubby grass, listening.

Her foot sank into a leaf-covered hole. 'Ow!'

There was a great flapping of wings, and a large

black bird flew away.

A tall man in a waxed jacket and black wellies emerged from behind a tree. 'Thanks, I was watching that.' At the sound of his voice, Julie recognised Neil. His hair stuck out from under a khaki beanie. He frowned slightly. 'You all right, Julie? You haven't twisted your ankle, have you?'

'No. Um, sorry for disturbing you.' She registered the binoculars in his hand. 'You're a birdwatcher?'

'A birder, yes.' He raised his eyebrows. 'What are you smiling at?'

'Nothing,' said Julie, straightening her face. But he hadn't been exactly complimentary about her new hobby. 'I just didn't have you down as one of those people who stare at birds for hours.' Now that she thought of it, with his baggy jumpers, long legs and wild hair, Neil reminded her of a large, rather unkempt bird. The corner of her mouth crept up.

'Each to their own,' said Neil.

'You look as if you're dressed for an expedition.'

'It blends in with the background,' he said, unabashed.

Why aren't men ashamed of their hobbies, thought Julie. *Then again, why am I?* 'What sort of bird were you watching?' she asked.

'I was hoping for a woodpecker,' he said. 'I thought I saw one through the trees, but it didn't show itself. Although I did see a raven: the bird that just flew away. And all sorts of tits and sparrows and whatnot. Normally I go to the nature reserve on Saturdays but I don't have time today, so this will have to do.' He smiled. 'Anyway, enough about me and my funny habits. What brings you to the park on this chilly day? Stretching your legs?'

'Kind of,' said Julie. Then honesty got the better of her. 'I'm still trying to find the postbox topper. We're making another one, but… I suppose I want closure.'

'Oh.' She expected him to laugh or smirk, but he didn't. 'Good luck with that.' He looked at his watch. 'I'd better go, but if I spot anything or get any bright ideas, I'll let you know.' He raised his binoculars. 'Enjoy your walk.' Off he went, striding through the leaf-mould to the path and away.

Julie watched him go, her hand resting on the gnarled bark of a nearby tree. *It's kind of him to offer to help.* Her stomach rumbled. *It's time for me to go, too.*

She picked her way carefully back to the path, avoiding the now-obvious hole, and meandered towards the village. As she approached the gate, her eye caught a speck of yellow. Her heart leapt. Could it be…?

It was the bud of a miniature daffodil, bright against the stone post. *Oh well*, thought Julie. Nevertheless, that little yellow speck made her feel better. She wasn't sure why, but it did.

5

Julie felt considerably less well-disposed towards daffodils after several attempts to crochet one. The bit she'd done under Lucy's supervision in the library had been absolutely fine. That, however, was the easy part.

'How on earth did she make six of these?' she exclaimed, as she paused the YouTube video on her phone yet again and tried to rewind it to the right bit. She found what she wanted – or rather a few seconds before – but the ball of yarn wormed its way off her lap and rolled under the armchair. She tugged the end, which sent the ball further out of reach. She considered leaving it there, then considered the possibility of dust and spiders.

Julie paused the video, said a rude word quite loudly to relieve her feelings, put down her crochet and ferreted beneath the chair. The yarn came out with a bit of fluff attached, but nothing worse. She sighed, picked up the crochet and found the hook had detached itself so that she managed to undo the last three stitches. 'Aaargh!' She regarded the twisted mess, which reminded her of a miniature yellow alien, said another rude word, and went to make tea.

When Thursday evening came round, it found Julie in her armchair, crocheting and muttering. 'You can do this,' she told herself. 'You've made two of these ridiculous things and you've got a quarter of an hour to finish this one.' She glared at it. 'Watch out,' she told it, 'or you won't get your full complement of petals.'

The daffodil's trumpet regarded her insolently. 'Never again,' she said. 'Once I've made six of you, that's it. Daisies all the way next time.' She looked at her watch and continued to crochet.

As the minutes ticked away, her hook went faster and faster. Somehow, it acquired a will of its own, but in a good way. 'Come on,' she urged it. Then she realised she was talking to a crochet hook and remained silent until she completed the last stitch.

Carefully she fastened off and finished the daffodil, working the end of the yarn through the stitches. She dropped the flower on the coffee table. 'Yesss!' She threw her hands in the air. 'Free at last!' She glanced at the clock. 'And late!' She sprang up, stuffed the flowers and her materials in their bag, then ran to the little vestibule and shrugged on her coat.

As she was heading down the path, a door opened nearby. 'Er, Julie?' It was Neil's voice.

'I'm in a rush!' she cried. 'Can it wait?'

'Um, yes, I—'

'Great!' She gave him two thumbs up and hurried off.

***

Julie burst into the library, red-faced and panting. 'Sorry I'm late, I was finishing a daffodil.'

'I was about to message you,' said Vix, looking slightly cross. 'I wondered where you were.'

'Sorry,' said Julie. 'I got carried away. It's only five past, though.'

'How are you finding the daffodils?' asked Lucy.

'Honestly? Awful.'

Lucy laughed. 'They are, aren't they? I finished them out of a sense of duty. I must admit, I was glad when you volunteered to take them on.'

Julie grimaced. 'Thanks for nothing.' She saw an empty seat next to Tegan and hurried round the table. 'How is everyone?'

Bernie shrugged. 'Plodding on.' She looked at the postbox hat, which was starting to take shape. 'I meant to get more done, but— I haven't been in the mood.'

'I know what you mean,' said Tegan. 'Spite and bloodymindedness are keeping me going. I'm not

43

letting the evil killer ducks beat me.'

Miriam laughed. 'That's the spirit.' Then her face grew serious. 'If people aren't feeling it, we don't have to make another topper. We can move on and do something else.'

'Absolutely not,' said Julie. 'I haven't sweated over these flaming daffodils to give up now.'

'I suppose there's no news of the topper,' said Bernic, wistfully.

'Sorry,' said Julie. 'I can't think of anything else to do. My neighbour said he'd keep an eye out – he's a birdwatcher so he's got binoculars.' Vix snorted. 'But I've mostly been swearing at these things in my spare time.' She took a daffodil out of her bag and shook it.

'Oh wow,' said Lucy, peering at it. 'That looks good. I kept going wrong with mine and having to unpick them.'

'They're so fiddly,' said Julie. 'Aren't you?' she asked the daffodil, and made it nod.

Tegan shuddered. 'That reminds me of a nightmare I had. Please don't make it talk.'

Julie gave her a sidelong glance and put the daffodil away.

She managed another half daffodil at the session. Every so often, she glanced around the table. Everyone was working steadily, but the mood was subdued. When they were working on the first topper there had been laughter and chat. Now there was quiet, slightly grim determination.

'How are we getting on?' Miriam asked, looking up from a half-finished crocus. 'Not that I'm hurrying you: I just want to get an idea of where we are.'

'Three and a half daffodils,' said Julie. 'And not a great deal of sanity.'

'Two killer ducks,' said Tegan.

'I'm dying to say a partridge in a pear tree,' said Natalie. 'Really, it's one and a half lambs.'

The list went round the table. Vix had produced an army of small yellow chicks. 'If anyone needs a hand, I've got capacity,' she said. 'Jules, are you managing OK?'

'I'm over halfway,' said Julie. 'I'm not going to be defeated by a flipping daffodil.'

'That's what we want to hear!' cried Vix, beaming. 'Stay *positive*, Jules.'

It's Julie, and you know that, Julie thought.

'So if we keep going at the same rate,' said Miriam, 'we could get the bits for the topper pretty much finished by the end of next week's session. Shall we aim for that?'

'Yeah, why not,' said Tegan.

Bernie interlaced her fingers and stretched her arms in front of her. 'I must admit, I'll be relieved to get it done. I found a fantastic pattern for a gorilla and I can't wait to make him.'

They parted at the door of the library with

goodbyes and Julie set off for home. It had gone chilly, more than she expected from mid-February. Then again, she hadn't been out at night for a long time. She zipped her coat right up to the top, stuck her hands in her pockets and walked faster.

She was about to head down her garden path when she remembered that Neil had wanted to speak to her earlier and went to knock on his door.

She was still waiting a minute later. *He can't have gone to bed*, she thought. *It's nine fifteen. And there are lights on, so presumably he's in.*

She saw movement behind the etched-glass panel in the door, followed by a dark shape looming closer, and it opened. 'Oh, hello,' said Neil. She was relieved to see he wasn't in his pyjamas, just another of his scruffy jumpers, teamed with black jeans. How many did he have? 'Sorry I took a while: I was working on something.'

'That's fine,' she said. 'You wanted to talk to me earlier?'

'Did I?' He looked puzzled. 'Oh yes, I wondered how you were getting on with the postbox top thingy.'

'The topper? Oh, we should finish it next week.'

'I meant investigating where the first one went. Have you made any progress?'

Julie sighed, puffing out a cloud of mist. 'To be honest, I've mostly been working on flowers for the new one.' She felt a pang of guilt. 'Thanks for asking, though.'

'It's just that I've had an idea.'

She stared at him. 'Have you?'

'I have!' He laughed, and she found herself smiling. 'It might be nothing, but I fell to wondering who on earth would bother to steal a postbox topper. No disrespect to the topper, you understand, but what else can you do with it? It's too big for a hat, the wrong shape for a tea cosy, and it's got weird stuff on it. Again, begging your pardon, all I could come up with was a rival knitter, or a group of them. Surely they're the only people who could possibly be interested.'

'I thought of something similar a while back,' said Julie, 'but I never followed it up. Someone in the group said they'd seen a postbox topper in Meadhurst. It's a faint possibility, but it's the first lead I've had. Thanks for reminding me, Neil.' She looked at her watch. 'I'll drive to Meadhurst now and do a recce. There can't be that many postboxes.'

'Now?' Neil's eyebrows shot up. 'Seriously?' He started laughing again. 'You could at least wait till it's light.'

He's got a point. 'Yeah, I suppose so,' said Julie. 'Fair enough, I'll head out early tomorrow and drive through Meadhurst on my way to work.'

'In that case,' said Neil, 'you'd better go and have your cocoa. Let me know how it goes.' He yawned.

'Sorry, too much staring at a screen. Probably time I knocked off.'

'You're still working?' It was Julie's turn to raise her eyebrows.

'Yup, got a deadline. That's the problem with working for yourself – the boss can be a right meanie.' He grinned.

'Well, I say you should take the rest of the day off, whatever your boss thinks.' She smiled back at him. 'Good night, Neil. And thanks.'

She walked down the path, then out by his garden gate, in by hers, and towards her own front door. *Silly, really. There ought to be a shortcut.* Neil was still in his doorway, so she waved and held up her keys. 'Don't worry, I can make it from here.'

'Night, Julie.' He went in.

Julie closed her door and leaned against it for a moment. Her heart was beating rapidly. *A lead*, she thought, *a proper lead! What if I find the postbox topper tomorrow?*

It's a slim chance, her more sensible self told her. *Does it matter, given that you're making another one anyway?*

That's not the point. I want to know. She went to put the kettle on, resolving to set her alarm for an hour earlier the next morning. 'The game is afoot,' she murmured.

6

Despite Julie's early alarm, she still woke half an hour before it went off. *Should I get up?*

Don't be silly, you won't be able to see anything. But she was wide awake and it was no use trying to doze. So she got up and made tea and toast, mulling over a plan of action. *What if I find the postbox topper?*

Bring it back, obviously.

What if someone sees me and thinks I'm stealing it? What do I do then?

Someone probably took a photo of it in the village.

But how do I prove it's the same one?

You can worry about that when you find it.

On impulse, she got her phone and looked in the WhatsApp group, but there were no photos of the postbox topper. *Why on earth didn't Miriam take one?*

With reluctance, she opened Facebook. She did

have a profile, but she barely used it. Some of the knitting group had mentioned craft projects they'd seen on Facebook, though, so maybe it was worth looking into. There was a village Facebook group: Neil had told her and Jason when they moved to Meadley. However, he'd said most of the posts were people moaning about speeding cars and young people on bikes. She found it – Meadley Village Chat – and scrolled through recent posts. Nothing. It was as if the postbox topper had never existed.

Julie closed her eyes and murmured 'It's real, I know it is.' She saw the time in the corner of her phone. *Honestly, stop woolgathering and get on with it.* She dressed warmly, in case she needed to leave the car somewhere and walk. Then she went to the kitchen drawer and took out a large pair of scissors which could cut through almost anything. 'Even if they've wired it on, I'll get it,' she muttered grimly. She pulled on a hat, got her keys and left, closing the door quietly in case Neil was up and doing. While it would have been useful to have another pair of eyes on the search, she could do without any wisecracks at her expense about following a trail of wool.

The roads were quiet. Julie usually left for work early anyway, to avoid the traffic, but lit by the first rays of a nondescript dawn, the road felt ghostly. At least it was warmer: a balmy four degrees, according to the car.

She drove along the winding country road, gripping the steering wheel tight and watching for the sign announcing that she was entering Meadhurst. 'There it is,' she whispered. 'I have to keep a lookout now.' And she slowed down.

Meadhurst was bigger than she remembered – not quite a town, but certainly a larger village than Meadley. She drove carefully, alert for a splash of red. Not that it would be bright red in this light, more a dark reddish-grey. *You mug. Why are you doing this? There must be someone else who could come here during the day.* She thought she saw something and her heart missed a beat. Then she realised it was a small red car and released her pent-up breath.

She came to what she remembered as the village centre, a sort of crossroads. *It does have a post office, doesn't it? If Meadley has one, surely this place does.*

There's only one way to find out. Julie turned left and drove slowly, glancing from side to side as if she was watching a long tennis rally at Wimbledon. Soon the shops, pubs and restaurants petered out, giving way to rows of houses and the occasional small apartment block. She found a safe place to turn round. *Maybe the next road.* At the crossroads, she took another left.

It was getting lighter. A postbox would be easier to spot. And she did spot one, but the postbox wore no topper, standing bald and proud outside the post office in the growing winter light. 'Damn,' said Julie, through gritted teeth. She kept going, looking for a side road, but there was a car behind her and it was a few minutes before she could safely turn round.

At the junction, she took the last arm of the crossroads. No postbox was there. *At least I tried*, she thought, and searched for somewhere to pull in.

As she turned into a pub car park, a horrible thought struck her. What if someone in Meadhurst *had* stolen the topper, but put it on a postbox in a side road? Or even hidden it? *They wouldn't do that. The whole point of a postbox topper is to have it where everyone can see it.* Nevertheless, the thought nagged her as she drove back to the crossroads.

Off to work, I suppose. She took the road for Meadborough. The car's clock said it was twenty past eight. She sighed. Normally, she was in work for eight thirty. But she always worked her hours, at least, and it wasn't as if she *had* to be in that early. It was just a habit. Nevertheless, she accelerated until she was driving at the speed limit. Then she glanced at the passenger seat. Her bag wasn't there. She huffed, and smacked the steering wheel lightly. *You idiot, Julie.*

What will I do for lunch? She remembered the ham salad sandwich she had made the night before, which was sitting in the fridge. And her purse was in the bag. Her phone was at home too, and sometimes work contacts rang or messaged her on it.

She growled, took the next side road, and found herself doing a seven-point turn.

Now, of course, everyone was going to work or dropping their kids at school. Every traffic light turned red as Julie approached it, but finally, thankfully, she reached her street and parked outside her house. She dashed in, grabbed her things, and pulled the door closed.

As she was locking it, Neil's front door opened. 'Hello there,' he called. 'Have you been topper hunting? I heard the squeal of wheels and smelt burning rubber.'

In spite of herself, Julie laughed. 'I have, but I didn't find one.' She advanced to the low fence which separated their gardens. 'I drove all round the main part of Meadhurst and I only found one postbox, never mind one with a hat on. I figured it wasn't worth searching the side streets because...'

'Because what?' said Neil, but Julie paid him no attention. Her gaze was fixed on something by Neil's shin. A jute shopping bag with a glimpse of soft, sickeningly familiar colours at the top: pale green, white and yellow.

'Wait right there.' She marched along her path then down Neil's, gathering momentum with every step. 'It was you, wasn't it?' She pointed an accusing finger, which to her annoyance trembled slightly. 'You, all the time. Why, Neil? What have I ever done to you?

53

Why can't I have hobbies? Don't I deserve them? Aren't I *allowed* to enjoy myself? You've been laughing behind my back, haven't you? Asking me about the topper and sending me on a wild-goose chase!'

Neil took a step back. 'I'm not sure what you— '

'It's right there!' If she could have stabbed him with her finger, she would have. 'You haven't even bothered to hide it. I bet you've enjoyed standing at the door chatting with me, knowing it's two feet away.'

Neil's gaze followed the direction of her finger. Slowly, he picked up the bag, drew out a ball of white wool and dropped it on the floor. Then a yellow one, then a green. His face was expressionless.

Julie stared at them, then him. 'What— '

'I was in the charity bookshop in Meadhurst – checking out a book about birds, surprisingly enough – and they had wool in. It looked like the right colours for your new postbox topper, so I bought some. When I told the manager what it was for, she gave me a discount: turns out she lives in Meadley. I meant to give it to you – that's why it's by the door – but work's been busy and I forgot.' He swiped the balls of wool from the floor, dropped them in the bag and thrust it at her. 'You might as well take it; I've no use for it. Now, if you'll excuse me.' He pulled the door to smartly, not looking at her.

Julie stood nonplussed, the bag of wool in her arms. Slowly, she bent and opened the flap of the letterbox. 'Neil, I'm sorry.' Her voice was shaking. *For heaven's sake.* 'I have to go to work. I'm late already.'

Silence.

'I really am sorry, but it did look like...' She let the letterbox flap fall and trailed down the path to her car.

She arrived at work just after nine, but all the parking spaces near the building were taken. It took her ten minutes to find a parking space and reach her office, where she found her boss perched on her desk, arms folded. 'Why are you so late, Julie?'

She consulted her watch. 'I know I'm later than usual, Greg, but the flexitime policy says—'

'You're always in for eight thirty. Not that it matters normally, but I've had complaints.'

She froze. 'A complaint?'

'Not *a* complaint. Complaint*sss*.' He actually hissed at her. 'Yes. That report you were meant to go through. When I sent it out yesterday afternoon, I didn't expect to come in this morning to a load of emails from our clients pointing out multiple errors.'

'What kind of errors?'

'The point is, Julie, you're meant to make sure reports are error free *before* I send them.'

'I made lots of corrections,' she said, in a daze.

'Not enough. I don't want jokey little emails from my clients saying *Not up to your usual high standard* or *Someone's having an off day*. From what I understand, you've had more than one off day lately. I heard on the grapevine that you've joined some sort of ladies' knitting circle and you've been getting excited over a stupid *postbox* hat. What you do in your own time is your business, but when it starts affecting your work, you'd better think on. Do I make myself clear?'

'Yes.' It was almost a whisper.

He leaned forward. 'What was that?'

'Yes, Greg. Sorry, Greg.' She swallowed. 'I won't let it happen again.'

'Make sure you don't.' The desk creaked as he rose. 'There won't be a formal sanction this time, but if it happens again...' He gave her a contemptuous look and walked out.

On autopilot, Julie hung up her things, sat down and switched on her computer. She stared at the company logo on her screen, then got up, closed the door and put her face in her hands, hoping nobody could hear her crying.

7

Eventually, Julie made herself a strong cup of tea and dared to face her email. She'd already checked her phone, which had been on silent, and seen various messages from Greg.

8:40: *Where are you? I want a word*

8:52: *Are you all right? I checked your work calendar and you ought to be in by now*

8:59: *Please report to me as soon as you get in*

9:05: *Has something happened? I rang but the phone went to voicemail. I left a message. Ring me asap*

Julie listened to the message. *Hi, Julie, it's Greg. Your boss. Wondering where you are. We need to talk. Hope you're OK, I'm a bit worried. Right, yes, bye.*

She bit her lip and deleted it. *What a morning. I've*

managed to annoy my boss, make a complete fool of myself and wrongly accuse Neil. He'll probably never speak to me again. She remembered his face as he had dropped the wool on the floor, and sighed. *He did something nice for me and I thought the worst of him.*

At the top of her email inbox was a message headed *MANDATORY FIRE TRAINING – OVERDUE.* Apparently, she ought to have completed the online training module by the previous Friday. 'Silly me,' murmured Julie. She wasn't in the mood for clicking her way through a series of questions she could have answered in her sleep. But a quiz she could do in her sleep was probably the safest option on a day like today. The worst that could happen was that she had to redo the module. She glanced through the rest of her email in case there was anything urgent, then clicked the link.

Q1: What sort of fire extinguisher should you use in the event of an electrical fire?
A: foam
B: water
C: carbon dioxide

Julie clicked C and pressed *Submit.*

Correct! Well done! Are you ready for the next question?

Julie huffed and selected *Yes*.

She clicked her way through the questions and achieved a score of 85%, which the system told her was a pass. *There's room for improvement though, Julie. Would you like to retake the test?*

Julie rolled her eyes and clicked the button which said *No, thanks*.

That done, and a certificate printed for her records, she sipped her cooling tea and closed her eyes. *I should go and apologise properly to Greg. He was actually worried about me.*

She finished her drink and stood up just as someone knocked on the door. 'With you in a minute,' she said, and inspected herself in the pocket mirror she kept in her bag. She was still a bit red around the eyes, but otherwise appeared pretty much as normal. 'Come in!'

Greg put his head round the door, looking sheepish. 'I came to say sorry.'

'Oh.' She managed a smile. 'I was about to come and do the same thing.'

'Ah. Mind if I sit down?' He eyed the chair in front of her desk.

'Of course you can.' She resumed her seat behind the desk. This was odd. Usually she went to see Greg. Now, it almost felt as if she was the boss. What a thought.

'I didn't mean to have a go at you earlier,' he said.

'I hadn't even noticed the errors in the report until I started getting emails pointing them out. A few typos, that was all.'

Julie shrugged. 'I'm sorry I missed them. As I said, I'll do my best to make sure it doesn't happen again. If in future I think I'll be in much past eight thirty, I'll send a message. I'm sorry you were worried, Greg. And I'll make sure my phone isn't on silent.'

'Thanks.' Greg shifted in his seat. 'It was what your friend said that wound me up. And worried me.'

'My friend? Do you mean Vix?'

'Very enthusiastic, tall and a bit chunky, works in sales. Don't tell her about the chunky bit.'

'That would be her.' Curiosity got the better of Julie. 'What did she say?'

'I didn't go seeking her out, you understand. I saw her in the corridor this morning and asked if she knew where you were. She launched into this big spiel about how she'd invited you to her knitting group because you were so sad and lonely and you were trying to track down a – a missing postbox topper?' He sounded as if he was attempting to speak a foreign language he'd never studied. 'She said you'd become obsessed with it and you didn't have anything else to live for.' He huffed out a breath. 'That's what worried me. I thought you might have—'

'*Me?*' Julie stared at him. 'Things aren't that bad.

OK, I'm not partying every night, but—'

'I hope I haven't spoken out of turn,' said Greg. 'I'm sure she means well.'

'I daresay she thinks she does,' Julie said grimly. She clenched her hands into fists, realised what she was doing, and clasped them instead.

Greg scrutinised her with a frown. 'You still look pale,' he said. 'I'm not sure you should be in work today.'

'I'm fine. I've done my fire training and everything.'

He peered at the certificate. '85%? That's definitely a sign you're not right.'

'It's still a pass,' Julie countered. 'It'll do.'

It was his turn to stare at her. 'You never think like that. You *never* let anything go. That's probably what your friend means about this postbox business. I bet you've been spending every hour outside work looking for the damn thing, whatever it is. I'm used to you picking through everything, holding us to account and keeping us on target. You're a machine.'

She raised her eyebrows. 'Am I? A machine?'

'I didn't mean it like that. I meant you're great at it, and I value that immensely. It's— This line of work is very competitive. We need to be the best just to survive, and you're a big part of that. Even tiny little errors make a difference.' Greg ran a hand through his short, greying hair, and Julie suddenly realised that he seemed a fair bit older than he had when she joined the company three years before. 'You should head home. You look terrible.'

'Thanks,' said Julie, with a wry smile.

'Can someone come and fetch you? I'm not sure you should be driving. Or maybe your friend could—'

'I'm fine to drive,' Julie said firmly.

Greg looked dubious. 'I'd take you, but I'm in a meeting in ten minutes.' His face cleared. 'I'll get reception to ring a taxi for you. Take a, what is it, a mental health day. It's Friday anyway, nothing ever happens on a Friday. Your car will be fine in the car park.'

'Yes, but—' For a second, Julie thought of phoning Neil. She had his number in her phone, for emergencies. *That ship has sailed,* she thought sadly. 'OK.'

'Great.' Greg stood up and rolled his shoulders. 'It'll do you the world of good.'

'Maybe you're right.' Julie logged off her computer and packed her bag. *At least my lunch had a nice trip in. I can fetch the car later, when Greg is taking his usual Friday long lunch.*

***

Julie spent the taxi ride home analysing various bits of the conversation she had had with Greg. 'Machine, indeed,' she muttered.

'Sorry, love?' said the taxi driver.

'Nothing, sorry.' *And as for Vix...* She scowled. *Am I being too hard on her? Am I obsessed? I suppose I am lonely, but I'm not sad. Not all the time, anyway. And I'm a lot less sad than I was. I have Vix to thank for that. If she hadn't invited me to the group—*

None of this would have happened, said a precise voice in her head.

I wouldn't have enjoyed myself spending time with the group and learning a new skill, Julie insisted. *And I'm grateful. Vix isn't perfect, but she means well. You can't expect people to be perfect.* Neil flashed into her mind, with his long hair, his dry humour, his scruffy jumpers and his silly birdwatching clothes. Not that they were silly, in context. *I'm not perfect, far from it. Maybe I should accept that.*

'What number is it, love?' asked the driver.

'Thirty-two.'

The taxi slowed to a stop. 'Very nice,' the driver said, approvingly. 'Got your things?'

'I think so.' Julie checked her bag. Then she considered the question more broadly. *You have a home, a job, friends, a hobby...* She closed her eyes for a moment and saw Neil, smiling at her. *You have everything you need, if you'd only see it.*

She thanked the driver and got out, then steeled herself and opened Neil's gate.

He might be out, she thought, as she walked down the path.

She knocked and waited. *He might be busy working. He said he had a deadline.*

Or he might be ignoring you.

She waited another minute, then knocked again, harder.

'Scuse me, love.' The taxi driver was leaning out of his window. 'Should I hang on? It's just that I've got another job to go to.'

'Oh no, please go. I live in the house next door. I don't think he's in, anyway.' She jerked her thumb at the door and it opened. Neil stood in the doorway, his hair wet and his T-shirt on inside out. Julie blinked, twice.

'I was in the shower,' he explained. 'What's happened? Why have you come home? You never do that during the day. You haven't—'

'I'll let you two get on,' said the driver, grinning. He closed his window and moved off slowly.

Julie turned to Neil. 'I'm so sorry about earlier. I can explain.' Water was dripping onto the shoulders of his T-shirt, which clung to him. She had a sudden vision of him in the shower that made her take a step back. 'I'm sorry I disturbed you. I should go.'

'You look as if you need a cup of tea,' said Neil. He opened the door wider and stood aside, and she walked into the house.

8

'As I said, I'm really sorry, and I should have thought before jumping in and accusing you of—'

Neil held up a hand. 'You can stop apologising, Julie. I get it: you made a mistake and you're sorry. I accept your apology. And I can see why you jumped to conclusions.'

'The wrong concl—'

He laughed. 'Have you finished that tea yet?'

Julie glanced at the inch or so of tea in her mug. 'Almost.' She drained it. 'I'm sorry. You must have work to do, and here I am in your sitting room unburdening myself.' Neil's sitting room was surprisingly nice, with a large squashy sofa, a colourful rug on the wooden floor, and modern art prints on the cream walls. She had already checked the bookcase for mystery novels. *Nobody's perfect.*

Neil smiled. 'As it happens, I don't have any work

to do. Not that won't wait. The deadline for the thing I was working on is at noon today, but I got it in yesterday evening. I hate leaving things till the last minute.'

'Do you? I do too.' She hadn't seen Neil as particularly organised. It was probably the hair and the jumpers.

'I may look like a scruffy herbert,' said Neil, 'but I'm actually quite business-minded. Anyway, what I was going to say, before we went off on a tangent, was that I'm heading to the nature reserve for a walk and a bit of birdwatching. I wondered if you wanted to come.'

'Me?'

He laughed. 'Yes, you. I mean, if you have other things to be getting on with—'

'No, not at all.' She put her mug on the coffee table. 'It's just that I can identify a blackbird and that's about it.'

'Oh dear,' said Neil. 'The nature reserve won't let you in if you fail the bird test.'

'The bird te— Oh.' She giggled, which surprised her. 'Are you sure you don't mind?'

His eyebrows drew together for a moment. 'I wouldn't have invited you if I minded, would I?' He eyed her work shoes. 'Although maybe you should change your shoes. There could be puddles.'

'OK.' Julie stood up. 'I'll give you a knock in five

minutes.'

At home, she put her lunch in the fridge and ran upstairs. The jumper she had on was fine, but the knee-length skirt would be ridiculous in a nature reserve. She changed into jeans, brushed her hair, then went to the bathroom and washed her face. Would it be overkill to put on make-up? She checked her watch. *It won't matter if I'm a minute late*, she thought, and reached for her mascara.

Neil gave her trainers an approving look. 'Right, let's go.' He'd put on similar clothes to the gear he'd worn in the park, but somehow it didn't seem silly now. He picked up a satchel. 'Where's your car, by the way? You came home in a taxi.'

'At work,' said Julie. 'My boss didn't want me to drive.' The minute she said it, she regretted the words. *He'll think I'm odd.*

'Don't see why,' said Neil. 'I can take you to fetch it later. So long as you promise not to ram me.'

'You'd better show me some good birds, then,' said Julie, and grinned.

Neil's car was small, and she was surprised when it moved without warning. 'Oh, it's electric,' she said.

'Yeah. Silent and sneaky.'

'I hadn't noticed.' There was so much she hadn't noticed, for such a long time.

The nature reserve was closer than Julie had realised. The sun had come out, and its rays did their best to get through the bare branches of the trees. 'We can do a loop of the hides,' said Neil. 'That way, hopefully you'll spot a variety of birds. Assuming they play ball.'

The first hide had posters on the walls with pictures of birds that frequented the nature reserve. Unfortunately, they were elsewhere that day. In the absence of birds, Neil taught Julie how to use the binoculars and she focused on different things: the bird feeder, a clump of snowdrops in a dell, another bird hide on the other side of the clearing. In the slit which served as a window she could see another birder in an army jacket, hiding behind a camera with a huge lens. 'The paparazzi are out,' she said, and handed Neil the binoculars.

He panned around the landscape. 'Oh yes. That'll be Frank the Flash.' He lowered the binoculars. 'You're pretty good with these.'

Julie was about to say that she'd seen Frank by chance, then checked herself. 'Thanks. I had a good teacher.'

'Flattery will get you everywhere,' said Neil. 'Let's try another hide. The birds must be somewhere. Not the one Frank's in, though: he'll shush you if you talk.'

They left the hide and strolled. Julie had expected Neil to be the sort of man who strode away and left you to catch up, but he walked as if there was plenty of time. 'What is it you do?' she asked. 'I know you work from home, and that you work for yourself.'

'I'm an environmental consultant,' said Neil. 'Building firms come to me when they're planning a new housing estate or retail park and I advise them on what to do to maintain local biodiversity.'

'Oh, right.'

'I used to work in an office, at a collar-and-tie sort of job, but I decided to go it alone after my wife ran off with her boss.'

Julie's eyes widened. 'I'm so sorry. I didn't mean to poke my nose in.'

'You didn't, I told you. It was five years ago: I'm over it now. We had to sell the house, of course, so I chose to find somewhere smaller than the fancy place we'd been struggling to pay for and do what I wanted for a change.'

'I don't blame you.' She blinked. She had always assumed Neil was a confirmed bachelor – in other words, grumpy and set in his ways. How had they never had a conversation like this before, in three years of living next door to each other? *You know why. You were too busy dealing with your own pain. Or not.*

'How about you?' he asked. 'What made you move to Meadley?'

'It was my – it was Jason's idea and I went along with it. It was meant to be a step towards retirement.

Not that I don't like Meadley: it's very nice. But it's difficult to leave the place and the people you know.'

'It is. I didn't realise until after we broke up how much stuff we did as a couple, and how much of a spare part I felt as a single man. Anyway, enough reminiscing. Let's try this hide.'

The second hide was more basic, and without posters. They opened the wooden flaps that covered the window slots and got comfortable on the high wooden bench. 'Here.' Neil passed Julie the binoculars. 'You have first go and tell me what you see.'

'OK.' Julie took the binoculars, hung the strap round her neck, and focused. 'Bird on the lake, black with a white bit on its head. Don't know what that is.'

'That's a coot,' said Neil. 'Any ducks?'

'No ducks,' said Julie, 'not even killer ones.' She could feel Neil staring at her. 'Sorry, that's a crochet joke.'

'You're a wild bunch when you get together, you lot.'

'Like you wouldn't believe.' She panned up. 'Oh, there's a bird on a feeder… Is it a blue tit?' She described it.

'That sounds about right.'

'It's flown off.' Julie scanned the landscape for anything else of interest. 'A black bird flew towards the trees. Not a blackbird, a black bird, and it's…

70

Wait.' She turned the focusing wheel. 'It can't be.'

'A black bird might be a crow or a raven,' said Neil. 'Then again, it might just be a big blackbird.'

Julie continued to stare through the binoculars. 'Near the top of a tree, there's something green and blue with little bits of white and yellow.' She fought to keep her voice steady. 'Could you have a look, please? To make sure I'm not hallucinating.' She gripped the binoculars tightly, ducked out of the strap and gave them to Neil.

'Let's see.' She watched his profile as he gazed through the binoculars. His eyes crinkled at the corners as he focused. He said nothing for a few seconds, then lowered the binoculars. 'Yup,' he said, 'that's a pair of ravens. I think I said I'd seen one the other day, in the park. They've pinched your postbox topper for their nest.'

Julie stared at him, then started laughing.

'You're taking it pretty well,' said Neil, smiling.

'I'm not climbing up there for it!' She grinned at him. 'At least they're making good use of it. And it's nice that nobody stole it. No human, anyway.'

'This is true,' said Neil.

'Wait till I tell the group,' she said. 'They won't believe it. It's a shame we can't get a photo. I don't think my phone can manage it.'

'I doubt mine can, but I know the man to ask. Come on, let's find Frank.' Neil put the caps on his binoculars and stood up.

'Why not,' said Julie. She followed him out of the hide, chuckling to herself.

9

'It gives me great pleasure to unveil the new Meadley village postbox topper.' The mayor pulled on the ribbon round the cloth-draped postbox and it fell to the ground. The cloth, however, didn't move.

Miriam and Bernie, who were standing nearby, lifted the fabric and revealed the topper.

'Ooo,' breathed the actually quite large crowd.

Tim from the paper (as Miriam had referred to him when persuading Julie that the tale of the postbox topper would make a brilliant story for the *Meadborough and District Times*) nudged the photographer, who snapped a few pictures. 'Now one with the knitting group,' Tim said. 'Come on, ladies. Let's have you gathered round the postbox.'

'Go on then,' said Neil, nudging Julie.

'Do I have to? I always look uncomfortable in photos, like I want to be somewhere else.'

'The paper wouldn't be here if it wasn't for you,' said Neil. 'You've only got yourself to blame.'

'All right,' said Julie. She stuck a smile on her face and walked forward.

'That's it, Julie, stand next to the postbox,' said Tim. 'Maybe point to the ravens.'

Tegan had been delighted when Julie told them the full story of the postbox topper at the next meeting. 'I love ravens!' she cried. 'They're so smart and black and Gothic, with all that croaking and nevermore. Right, I'm gonna make two ravens to go on the new topper.'

'Won't that look odd?' said Vix. 'They're not exactly springlike.'

'They'll be the only wildlife on the postbox topper that's actually been anywhere near it,' Tegan pointed out. 'Anyway, it's good practice for Halloween.' She fetched a ball of black yarn, plonked it on the table and pulled out her crochet hook with a determined air.

Miriam sighed. 'Don't make them too Gothic, Tegan.'

'Don't worry, they'll be cute.'

Julie, smiling for the camera, gave the ravens a sidelong glance. They weren't cute, exactly, but the nest between them, filled with knitted eggs, definitely softened the effect.

'Lovely,' called Tim. 'Julie, is your friend here? The chap who was with you when you found the postbox topper?'

Julie grinned. 'Oh yes.' She beckoned Neil. 'Come on, Neil, time for your moment of glory.'

'Not again,' said Neil, but she had already noted that the jumper he was wearing was one of his less baggy ones and he had definitely brushed his hair that morning.

'One on each side, George?' Tim asked the photographer.

'Let's have you standing together,' said the photographer, regarding them critically. 'Neil, can you stand behind Julie and maybe put a hand on her arm?'

Julie tried not to jump as Neil's hand touched her elbow. Even through the layers of coat and jumper, she felt it. She wouldn't have been surprised if her arm had glowed.

'Lovely. Say postbox topper.'

'Postbox topper!' they chorused, trying not to laugh.

'I defy the smartest of ravens to get that off,' said Miriam, once the photographer had finished. She tapped the wire which secured the topper round the postbox. 'That was excellent publicity for the group. Thanks to Julie.'

'Not to mention my new side hustle,' said Tegan. 'I've got five orders for life-size killer ducks, and two people have already enquired about ravens.'

'What are you calling your business again?' said

Bernie.

'Feminist Death Knits,' said Tegan.

'Ah,' said Bernie, 'of course. Well, I'd better make tracks. My grandson's coming for a sleepover and I need to hide everything breakable.'

'Yeah, bye,' muttered Vix, and hurried away.

'What's up with her?' asked Tegan, gazing at Vix's retreating back.

'It's a long story,' said Julie.

Vix had knocked on Julie's office door at ten to five the day before. 'Was it you who set Human Resources on me?' she asked, without preamble.

'No,' said Julie. 'I haven't said anything about you to anyone.' She wondered what on earth Greg had said.

'Huh,' said Vix. 'I was just trying to help, but *some* people don't appreciate it. I could do without being given a lecture on gossip and oversharing in the workplace and sent on team dynamics training.'

'I'm sorry about that,' said Julie, 'but I honestly haven't spoken to HR.'

Vix sniffed. 'Well, someone did, Jules. Enjoy your weekend.'

'It's Julie. Not Jules.'

Vix peeled herself off the doorframe, stepped out of Julie's office and shut the door, quite loudly.

'Hope you enjoy your weekend too,' called Julie, but there was no reply.

She was roused from her memory by Miriam clapping her hands. 'While you're still here – most of you – we'll be talking new projects at the group on Thursday. Julie has exciting news to share.'

Natalie's eyes widened. 'You can't tease us like that!'

'Just did,' said Miriam, grinning. 'Now, I've got kids to take swimming and I believe you have too, Natalie.'

Natalie checked her watch. 'Oh heck. Bye, everyone!' And she hurried off, Miriam's bombshell entirely forgotten.

'So what's the big news?' Neil asked, as they strolled towards home. 'I promise not to spill the beans.'

'It's really not that big,' said Julie.

'Knowing you, that probably means it's massive.'

She laughed 'It isn't. You'll probably think it's ridiculous.'

He stuck his hands in his pockets. 'Try me.'

'All right, I'm reducing my hours at work.'

'Wow, that is big. How come?'

'I thought about what you said, that I'm never at home during the day. You're right. I don't need to work full-time hours, and there are lots of other things I'd like to do with my time.'

Neil raised his eyebrows. 'Such as?'

'I've never been a hobby sort of person. I've

always been very into my work. I mostly went along with what Jason wanted to do. Maybe it's time to find out what *I* want to do. Plus an opportunity has come up.'

'Tell me more.'

'A company called Occasion Knits contacted me. They do commissions for events and launches and art installations. I think they got the wrong end of the stick, to be honest. They read the first article in the paper, which said I was a project manager, and they put that and the postbox topper together.'

'Sensible people, if you ask me.'

'Anyway, they asked if I'd do some ad hoc work with them on their bigger projects, managing the knitters and the products and so on. I tried to pass them on to Miriam, but she wasn't having any of it. Other villages have approached us about making postbox toppers for them, or talking to their knitting groups about where to begin. And I've offered to do spreadsheets for Tegan to help her keep on top of Feminist Death Knits. I'm even getting used to the name.' She smiled. 'Plus I want more time to crochet myself. So I'm moving to four days a week on a trial basis. My boss wasn't happy, but I told him it would improve my work-life balance.'

Neil pondered this as they walked. 'I reckon you'll be busier than before.'

'It's possible. Hopefully, in a good way. I decided

it was time for something new.'

'A fresh start?'

'Something like that.' They fell silent.

Julie stole a glance at Neil. It was nice to walk next to someone and feel as if you sort of belonged there. She would always love Jason, and always miss him, but it was time to move on. It had been a long, long winter, but now it felt as if spring was coming.

'I've been learning about ravens,' she said.

'Oh yes?' They were almost at the red telephone box which served as the local book swap. Neil fell in behind her, then caught her up once they had passed it.

'I knew about the ravens at the Tower of London, obviously, but I didn't know how smart they are. No wonder they managed to steal the postbox topper. Perhaps one created a psychological moment in the village which allowed the other one to steal the topper.'

Neil stared at her. 'Do you really think so? A postbox topper heist?'

'Who knows? It's a good story.'

'It is.'

They were almost home, and the pace had slowed somewhat. 'I read that they mate for life,' said Julie, casually. 'That's rather nice, if it's true.'

'I suppose it is,' said Neil. 'Although ravens are probably less complicated than humans.'

'Yes. Life's probably easier for ravens in that respect.'

The corner of Neil's mouth quirked up. 'I imagine so.'

'I'm glad I'm not a raven, though.' She moved a little closer, but kept walking.

'Me too. I'm not keen on heights, for one thing. And there are other reasons.' Neil's hand brushed hers.

Julie hesitated a moment, then touched Neil's hand. Gently, his fingers closed around hers. 'Could you fit a cup of tea into your busy schedule?' he asked.

She smiled up at him. 'I'd be delighted.'

Six months later...

Julie now works three days a week. One of her first projects took place in her front garden: removing a fence panel and creating a path between her house and Neil's. She and her team have created and delivered a zoo's-worth of woollen animals, a giant cobweb installation with matching spider, and a life-size knitted three-piece suite. Julie can recognise twenty-five different birds, and in her spare time she is making Neil a jumper that fits for Christmas.

Tegan's Feminist Death Knits are sold online and in gift shops throughout Meadborough and she has taken on another knitter. Julie has had to expand her original spreadsheets. The most popular items are ravens (particularly the deluxe edition with red eyes that light up), but Tegan still sells the occasional uterus. She is working on a design for a Halloween postbox topper.

Following the unveiling of the postbox topper, Hooked on Yarn acquired so many new members that Miriam had to find a larger venue. She coordinates several knitting groups in Meadborough and is talking about starting a nationwide knitting and crocheting network. She has also negotiated a discount on bulk yarn deliveries with a major supplier.

Vix still comes to the group occasionally, but she tends to sit with the new people. She says she is taking them under her wing.

Bernie completed her gorilla, which was immediately claimed by her grandson. He takes Bananas everywhere with him, and Bananas always receives compliments.

Lucy decided to make some easy-to-follow crochet videos, and now has her own YouTube channel.

The next time Jake had a food tantrum, Natalie offered him a plate of crocheted fish fingers, chips, peas and sweetcorn instead. He was so surprised that he shut up and ate his meal.

Greg suggested HR bring in duvet days and co-delivers a session on staff burnout to new managers. He's considering cutting his hours to four days a week.

Neil asked Julie to teach him how to knit. He makes squares in front of the TV and drops them off at the nature reserve for birds to line their nests with. He also writes a monthly column about birdwatching for the local paper. He's thinking of suggesting a birding trip to the Scottish Highlands next spring, but he's not sure Julie will be able to fit it in.

What To Read Next

First suggestion: if you enjoyed this book and you haven't already read *The Book Swap*, give it a try! Both books are set in the village of Meadley (hence the series name) and while strictly *The Book Swap* happens first, you can read the stories in any order. Here's the global link: http://mybook.to/BookSwap.

Tales of Meadley is a sideways move for me, as I usually write mysteries! However, I have more suggestions…

If you like modern cozy mystery with older characters and a spot of romance, you might like the *Booker & Fitch Mysteries* series I write with Paula Harmon.

As soon as they meet, it's murder!

When Jade Fitch opens a new-age shop in the picturesque market town of Hazeby-on-Wyvern, she's hoping for a fresh start. Meanwhile, Fi Booker is trying to make a living from her floating bookshop as well as deal with her teenage son.

It's just coincidence that they're the only two people on the boat when local antiques dealer Freddy Stott drops dead. Or is it?

The first book in the series, *Murder for Beginners*,

is at https://mybook.to/Beginners.

If you like contemporary books with books in them (so to speak), you might enjoy my *Magical Bookshop* series. This six-book series combines mystery, magic, cats and books, and is set in modern London.

When Jemma James takes a job at Burns Books, the second-worst secondhand bookshop in London, she finds her ambition to turn it around thwarted at every step. Raphael, the owner, is more interested in his newspaper than sales. Folio the bookshop cat has it in for Jemma, and the shop itself appears to have a mind of its own. Or is it more than that?

The first in the series, *Every Trick in the Book*, is here: http://mybook.to/bookshop1.

If you love modern cozy mysteries set in rural England, *Pippa Parker Mysteries* is another six-book series set in and around the village of Much Gadding.

In the first book, *Murder at the Playgroup*, Pippa is a reluctant newcomer to the village. When she meets the locals, she's absolutely sure. There's just one problem: she's eight months pregnant.

The village is turned upside down when a pillar of the community is found dead at Gadding Goslings playgroup. No one could have murdered her except the people who were there. Everyone's a suspect, including Pippa...

With a baby due any minute, and hampered by her

toddler son, can Pippa unmask the murderer?

Find *Murder at the Playgroup* here: http:// mybook.to/playgroup.

Acknowledgements

My first thanks go to my brilliant beta readers: Carol Bissett, Ruth Cunliffe, Paula Harmon and Stephen Lenhardt. Thank you for your feedback and suggestions! Any remaining errors are my responsibility.

I'm lucky enough to live in a village where craft is frequently on display. The bollards in the village centre acquired a Christmassy wrapping, there's a metal 'tree' outside the library decorated with knitting and crochet which changes with the seasons, and I've spotted more than one postbox topper on my walks. At one point I worried that some of my crochet projects in this story were too ambitious – then I checked online and realised that the sky's the limit!

And many thanks to you, dear reader! I hope you've enjoyed this story, and if you have, please consider leaving a short review or a rating on Amazon and/or Goodreads. Reviews and ratings help books find new readers.

COVER CREDITS

Font: Allura by TypeSETit. License: SIL Open Font License v1.10: http://scripts.sil.org/OFL.

Cover illustration by me (please see copyright page).

About Liz Hedgecock

Liz Hedgecock grew up in London, England, did an English degree, and then took forever to start writing. After several years working in the National Health Service, some short stories crept into the world. A few even won prizes. Then the stories started to grow longer…

Now Liz travels between the nineteenth and twenty-first centuries, murdering people. To be fair, she does usually clean up after herself.

Liz's reimaginings of Sherlock Holmes, the Magical Bookshop series, the Pippa Parker cozy mystery series, the Caster & Fleet Victorian mystery series and the Booker & Fitch mysteries (written with Paula Harmon) and the Maisie Frobisher Mysteries are available in ebook and paperback.

Liz lives in Cheshire with her husband and two sons, and when she's not writing or child-wrangling you can usually find her reading, messing about on Twitter, or cooing over stuff in museums and art galleries. That's her story, anyway, and she's sticking to it.

You can also find Liz here:

Website/blog: http://lizhedgecock.wordpress.com
Facebook: http://www.facebook.com/
lizhedgecockwrites
Twitter: http://twitter.com/lizhedgecock
Goodreads: https://www.goodreads.com/lizhedgecock

Books by Liz Hedgecock

To check out any of my books, please visit my Amazon author page at http://author.to/LizH. If you follow me there, you'll be notified whenever I release a new book.

The Magical Bookshop (6 novels)
An eccentric owner, a hostile cat, and a bookshop with a mind of its own. Can Jemma turn around the second-worst secondhand bookshop in London? And can she learn its secrets?

Pippa Parker Mysteries (6 novels)
Meet Pippa Parker: mum, amateur sleuth, and resident of a quaint English village called Much Gadding. And then the murders begin…

Booker & Fitch Mysteries (4 novels, with Paula Harmon)
Jade Fitch hopes for a fresh start when she opens a new-age shop in a picturesque market town. Meanwhile, Fi Booker runs a floating bookshop as well as dealing with her teenage son. And as soon as they meet, it's murder…

Caster & Fleet Mysteries (6 novels, with Paula Harmon)
There's a new detective duo in Victorian London . . . and they're women! Meet Katherine and Connie, two young women who become partners in crime. Solving it, that is!

Mrs Hudson & Sherlock Holmes (3 novels)
Mrs Hudson is Sherlock Holmes's elderly landlady. Or is she? Find out her real story here.

Maisie Frobisher Mysteries (4 novels)
When Maisie Frobisher, a bored young Victorian socialite, goes travelling in search of adventure, she finds more than she could ever have dreamt of. Mystery, intrigue and a touch of romance.

The Spirit of the Law (2 novellas)
Meet a detective duo – a century apart! A modern-day police constable and a hundred-year-old ghost team up to solve the coldest of cases.

Sherlock & Jack (3 novellas)
Jack has been ducking and diving all her life. But when she meets the great detective Sherlock Holmes they form an unlikely partnership. And Jack discovers that she is more important than she ever realised…

Halloween Sherlock (3 novelettes)

Short dark tales of Sherlock Holmes and Dr Watson, perfect for a grim winter's night.

For children

A Christmas Carrot (with Zoe Harmon)

Perkins the Halloween Cat (with Lucy Shaw)

Rich Girl, Poor Girl (for 9-12 year olds)

WHITE
RHINO
BOOKS

Printed in Great Britain
by Amazon